An Unexpected Halloween

T.O. SMITH

TRIGGER WARNINGS:

This book contains numerous triggers. Here is a list of triggers this book contains:

Dubcon

Exhibitionism

Degrading/name-calling

Stalker

Kidnapping

Group sex WITHOUT sharing

PLEASE PROCEED WITH CAUTION.

For Riley, my reason for everything that I do.

And for every reader who has continued to follow me through my writing journey. I hope you all love this book as much as you love all of the others.

And also for every lover of extremely dark, fucked-up romance.

OTHER BOOKS IN THE SERIES

An Unexpected Halloween

An Unexpected St. Patrick's Day

Cover Design: Tiff Writes Romance

Editing: Tiff Writes Romance

Proofreading: Taylor Jade, Kimberly Peterson

Chapter One

Melanie was looking at me with pleading eyes, her blue-gray eyes almost enough to make me cave. I hated when she did this. Every time she looked at me with those puppy dog eyes, I eventually gave in to what she wanted.

And I really wasn't wanting to cave with this, more so than any other time my friends had pleaded with me to do something with them.

My friends - Melanie, Kylie, Jess - and my roommate, Amber had been trying to convince me to go to a party with them out at Canyon Lake.

Not just any party, though. A Halloween party.

I had strict rules against Halloween parties. I didn't do them. I had a superstition about bad things happening on Halloween night. I preferred to stay inside where I *knew* I was safe from psychos and all of the other crazies in the world.

And sure, Canyon Lake seemed like fun. In fact, normally, Canyon Lake *was* fun. It was a huge tourist destination in Texas, not to mention, even people who lived in this state - like us - loved it. Canyon Lake was a one-of-a-kind beauty, and the scenery leading to Canyon Lake was just as beautiful. The rolling hills and the countryside were a one-of-a-kind sight.

"You *need* to come to this party, Blaire," Melanie pleaded.

I sighed. I already hated parties, and my friends knew how I felt about this night in particular. "Melanie, you *know* how I feel about going out on Halloween night," I reminded her.

She huffed. I almost smiled. "But Blaire, it's our senior year!" she complained. "Can't you come out just this *once*?"

I almost scoffed. *Just this once*. She used that phrase every time she wanted me to go somewhere, and normally, I ended up going.

I shook my head at her. I refused to cave on this. "What if we promise to never leave your side?" Jess spoke up. I narrowed my eyes at her. It didn't matter what party we went to, we all somehow always got separated.

"Did you seriously just ask that?" I deadpanned.

Kylie grabbed my hand. She was normally quiet when our friends tried to get me to join in on the fun. I think it was because she tried to respect my boundaries, but I guess today, she really wanted me to come along with them.

"Blaire, *please*," she pleaded. "You only live once."

"Yeah," I scoffed, "and I'd like that to be a long time."

Amber huffed and rolled her eyes as she hopped off her bed, landing on the balls of her feet. "Last-ditch effort, Blaire." I arched an eyebrow at her. "I'll buy you every season of that Hallmark show you like if you agree to come to this party."

Oh, God, she drove an extremely hard bargain.

She smiled because she knew she had broken through my barrier and had me exactly where she wanted me. I released a long, drawn-out sigh. "*Fine*," I groaned. "But if we get separated, I'm leaving," I warned them.

"Deal!" Melanie shrieked, bouncing up and down, making a clapping motion with her hands, but not actually clapping them together. "Now, we just need to take you shopping. You *have* to dress up."

I groaned. This just kept getting worse and worse. "Do I really?" I whined. "You know how much I hate dressing up."

"Correction," Kylie said. "You hate stepping out of your comfort zone."

I glared at her. She just smiled sweetly at me. Rolling my eyes, I looked back at Melanie. "I don't even have the funds to buy a costume," I confessed. They knew how tight money was for me. Being a foster kid hadn't been easy. Even worse was starting college with just enough money to my name to get me through the first year of college.

Textbooks were expensive as hell.

"We'll buy it for you," Melanie said with a shrug.

For them, it was always that simple. All of my friends had come from parents with money who were funding their college educations. None of them had to pull out student loans like I had. None of them worked, either.

I had to work, and half of everything I earned was put into the bank to never be touched until I had to purchase textbooks. The rest I had to put into food and other necessities.

"Come on," Amber said, linking her arm with mine. She gave my bicep a gentle squeeze and bumped her hip with mine, making me smile. "Come out of your head. It's going to be fun," she promised. "And it'll be good for you to get out."

I sighed. "You know this isn't my kind of thing, Amber," I reminded her as we followed Melanie, Jess, and Kylie out of the dorm room.

Amber shrugged. "Maybe not," she confessed, "but it's still good for you to get some fresh air anyway. Besides, it's *Canyon Lake*. I know how much you love Canyon Lake."

Amber was my best friend. And sure, we were friends with Melanie, Jess, and Kylie, but Amber and I were the closest in the group. She had seen me at my worst so many times because of financial stress, and not once did she judge.

She took me to Canyon Lake for the first time during our freshman year, and I had fallen in love with the place. Despite it being so busy in the springtime because of the warmer weather, you still got a comforting feeling of solitude when you were surrounded by all those beautiful hills, the trees, the rocks, and that glistening, blue water.

I sighed. "You're right." Amber smiled widely at me. "Let's get this over with," I grumbled.

She laughed. "That's the spirit, Blaire!"

Spirit Halloween was a nightmare.

I already hated going out shopping as it was - even for groceries.

Stepping into Spirit Halloween on Halloween, nonetheless, was a catastrophe.

Melanie, Jess, and Kylie dispersed, going to grab last-minute things for their costumes. I glanced at Amber who was looking around the store like she needed something, though she had said she was good on everything. "You're sure you don't need to grab anything?" I asked Amber.

She shook her head. "I knew this place was going to be a disaster the closer it got to Halloween, so I grabbed everything I needed for my costume as early as possible," she explained.

At least she was smart enough to grab everything ahead of time. Looking around me, it didn't seem like everyone else was smart enough. Hell, the only reason I was here was because I'd kind of gotten forced into going to the party out at Canyon Lake.

"Do you have any idea what you want to dress up as?" Amber asked.

"Myself?" I asked hopefully, looking around at all the costumes. God, there were some bizarre ones. Like, who the fuck dressed up as a *pickle*?

Amber snorted. "No such luck," she told me. I released a long, low groan, making her laugh. "You like gothic shit, right? Wanna dress up as a hot, scene girl?"

I shrugged. It wouldn't be totally out of my comfort zone, I guess. I was familiar with the style, considering I'd been one of the few to keep with that trend after it kind of died out.

Kind of pissed me off that what I was once sort of bullied for in middle school and high school was now becoming popular again.

Amber dragged me around the store, grabbing first a black tutu, then some fishnet stockings. After, she grabbed some colored hairspray cans. "What are those for?" I demanded, staring at the cans in horror.

"We're going to color your hair tonight for the party, silly."

“Um, no, we are not.” I reached forward to grab them from her, but she skipped backward, grinning at me. “Amber, you’re not putting that crap in my hair,” I told her, meaning it. She wouldn’t be swaying me on this.

“Live a little, Blaire,” she pleaded. “Tonight is about having *fun*. And this will wash out in the shower tonight when you come home - I promise.”

“Amber–"

She cut me off. “Hallmark show, remember?”

I cast her a look that very clearly said *fuck you*. She laughed and grabbed my wrist, pulling me around the store some more.

I only prayed that tonight went by super fast. I hadn’t even gone to the party yet, and I was already ready to get back to the safety of my dorm room where no one could bother me and psychos couldn’t do fucked up shit.

Bad things happened on Halloween night, and I had no urge to ever be a part of them.

Fuck you, Amber. You drive a damn hard bargain.

“Stop cursing me in your head,” Amber said without turning around to face me. “A deal is a deal.” She swiped her credit card and thanked the lady working the register before thrusting the bag at me. "You're going. That's final. Hate me tomorrow after you've had the time of your life."

Something curled in the pit of my stomach - something akin to dread . . . But was that also *excitement*?

I shook my head.

This Halloween store was making me lose my mind.

Chapter Two

The lake was crammed with people down by the water. I'd been enjoying the crisp, Autumn air on the drive here, and now, I could smell alcohol, beer, and sweaty bodies mixed in with it.

It was disgusting, to say the least.

I was still in the passenger seat, the windows rolled down, staring at the people down by the water. How their scents were already reaching me, I didn't know – especially with the cooler air. But I dreaded the thought of smelling them all up close.

How were people already sweaty, especially in this cool air?

Amber leaned in my window while Melanie, Jess, and Kylie went straight down to the party, heading straight for the person handing out drinks. I shook my head. That was dangerous. You *never* took drinks from strangers.

And so much for sticking together. Three of our friends had already dispersed, and I knew it was only going to be a matter of time before Amber located her boyfriend, and she snuck off with him for sex.

The two of them could barely keep their hands off each other.

"Come on, Blaire," Amber said, drawing my eyes to her again. "A deal's a deal, remember?"

I huffed and shoved open the door. She grinned triumphantly and grabbed my hand in hers after I shut the passenger side door, and she dragged me through the grass down to the sand. I was glad that I had worn boots because I had no urge to have sand all in my shoes. I could already see some people annoyed by it.

Amber's boyfriend located us pretty quickly, and he separated from his friends to come greet us. Amber beamed at him, leaning up on her tiptoes to plant a hot kiss against his mouth. I looked away, feigning interest in something else until they were done sucking each other's faces off.

"Come on; let's get you two some drinks," Derreck said, leading us towards the alcohol table. He looked over at me with a friendly smile on his face. "Surprised to see you actually came."

I rolled my eyes. "Your girlfriend drove a hard bargain."

Derreck was a decent guy. He was kind, and he treated Amber well. And unlike a lot of guys I had seen Amber date in the past, he made sure she stayed focused on school and helped her when she needed it. Amber had a bad habit of getting distracted, but he kept her on track.

I really hoped they ended up working out.

Derreck laughed. "Yeah, she tends to do that," he agreed, making Amber blush. He pressed a kiss to the top of her head before grabbing three unopened beers, handing the guy a twenty, telling him to keep the change. He popped the top off one and handed it to me. "I know you're not a beer person, but this is the safest."

At least he was smart.

We followed Derreck over to his group of friends. I stayed quiet, listening to everyone as they spoke. Music suddenly began to play, and everyone dispersed, going to dance, Amber and Derreck included.

I was left by myself, just as I knew I would be.

Sighing, I poured my beer out on the ground and tossed my bottle into a nearby trashcan that was off to the side of the party, out of the way. Hell, it was actually kind of dark over here. You would think someone would be smart enough to point headlights down by the trashcan.

My skin suddenly crawled, the hairs on the back of my neck rising. I straightened and swung around to see who was staring at me, but I saw nothing but trees. I swallowed nervously, that feeling of being watched still not going away.

Dread curled in the pit of my stomach.

I was ready to get the fuck out of here.

I went in search of Amber since she was the one with the keys, but I couldn't find her anywhere. She and Derreck weren't dancing anymore, and they weren't at either of their vehicles.

Their nasty asses probably went to go fuck in the woods or some shit.

But that eerie feeling of being watched still wasn't going away. In fact, it was getting stronger - as if whoever was watching me was drawing closer and closer.

I tried the door handle on Amber's car so I could get my phone, but of course, she had locked it. I couldn't blame her. Our purses were in here as well as our cellphones.

"Fuck," I whispered, my heart beginning to race in my chest.

That eerie feeling grew even stronger.

I searched the party again, finally spotting Melanie dancing against a guy I vaguely recognized from my physics class. Relieved, I began to walk towards her.

"Not so fast, doll."

I didn't have time to scream.

A hand clamped over my mouth, and the man's arm snagged around my waist, yanking my body back against his. Hot tears sprang to my eyes. Fear clawed at my throat. My heart was beating so hard that it *hurt*.

I was going to die.

This was why I didn't go out on Halloween night.

I thrashed as he carried me towards the woods, and I screamed for help, but it was muffled beneath his hand. No one heard me over the music. No one could spot me in the darkness.

I was fucked - completely, royally fucked.

I was going to die tonight.

Chapter Three

Though the man seemed kind of lanky - a bit on the skinny side - my thrashing around didn't seem to faze him one bit. He held strong, not even grunting when I kicked and elbowed him numerous times.

"Stop," he growled in my ear, his voice surprisingly deep. Immediately, I stopped thrashing, my wide eyes scanning the woods around us.

We were completely secluded. I could barely see the party anymore. I'd been so blinded by panic and the need to get away that I hadn't even realized how far he'd dragged me.

"I'm going to set you down. Don't run, do you understand me? I'm not a nice guy, Blaire."

Chills raced down my spine.

He knew my name.

"And if I run?" I squeaked.

He ran his nose along the column of my neck. My traitorous body *loved* it. My core clenched, my pussy tingling.

What the fuck is wrong with you, Blaire?!

I squeezed my eyes shut, my heart knocking hard against my chest. I wasn't crazy. I *couldn't* be crazy, right?

The rest of my family was - had been so crazy they were unfit to care for me when my parents passed. But I'd thought I was okay. I'd made it this far without any signs.

Do not cave, Blaire.

"I *always* catch my victims, Blaire," he whispered hotly in my ear.

A chill of both thrill and fear raced down my spine.

What the fuck was wrong with me?

He slowly released me. The chill in the air suddenly wrapped around me, making me miss the warmth his body had provided. Shoving that longing aside, I swung around to face him.

Instantly, the breath was knocked from my lungs.

He was not what I was expecting.

He had pale skin for Texas - like he didn't see a lot of sunlight. His eyes were a startling shade of blue -

almost electric. His black hair hung in his face, and I watched as he swished it to the side, revealing his eyes completely. They were lined with black eyeliner, making their blue color that much bolder. A lip piercing sat on the side of his perfect mouth, and an eyebrow piercing sliced through his dark brow.

He was my dream man walking.

Why did he have to be a fucking psycho?

My brain thankfully hadn't stopped working, though. I opened my mouth to scream, and he suddenly pulled a knife from his belt, pressing the tip against my throat before I could react.

I snapped my lips shut, whimpering quietly as I stared down at the shiny blade, the moon reflecting off of it.

"Scream, doll," he taunted, a cruel smile twisting his perfect lips. "I promise I'll slit your throat."

"Okay," I croaked. "No screaming. I swear."

I wanted help, but I also wanted to survive tonight.

He lowered the knife, and I finally drew air into my lungs. He slid it back into his belt, swishing his hair out of his eyes again.

"What do you want with me?" I finally managed to ask. I could still hear the party happening down below, but it was low. He'd dragged me a good distance away from everyone else.

Here, it was just him and I, and I hated that I got a fucking thrill out of it along with the fear.

I was losing my mind. That was the only reasonable explanation. Maybe I actually needed medication. Maybe I wasn't so different from my fucked up family, after all.

"I've had my eyes on you for weeks, Blaire." A chill raced down my spine at his words. A smirk twisted his lips, and I hated that it made him look deadly yet so beautiful all at the same time.

With beauty came pain.

Wasn't that the motto women lived by? Or at least something along those lines?

"Weeks?" I finally managed to utter.

He nodded.

I'd never even noticed someone following me, someone staring at me. Everything had felt *normal.* And I had a feeling the *only* reason I had sensed him tonight was because he *wanted* me to know that he was there - lurking, waiting for me.

"I want to play a game, Blaire," he said softly, his eyes running over me. Every nerve ending in my body lit up at the sensual look in his eyes.

A game.

I kept my eyes on his, terrified to know what this game he had in mind would entail.

He stepped closer to me and curled his hand around my neck. My panties became drenched. Why was I *wet?*

Was I seriously turned on by this crazy, psychotic shit?

He brought his face close to mine, his minty breath fanning across my skin. His lips just barely brushed mine, and I actually *whimpered*, needing more. A delicious smirk teased his perfect lips.

"Your body will get what it craves *very* soon, doll." My heart hammered against my breastbone at his words. My belly clenched.

My mind and my body were at war.

My body wanted this - wanted him - and my mind was screaming at me to get the fuck away from him.

"I want you to run, Blaire. I *love* the thrill of the chase," he whispered hotly against my ear. I barely bit back a moan at the erotic feeling.

"But you didn't want me to run a little while ago," I whispered, suddenly confused.

He brushed a feather-light kiss to the corner of my lips. I sucked in a sharp breath of air. *Oh, God, why did this psycho have to be so alluring?*

"Everything you do is under my command, doll." My nipples were so hard they hurt. "When I say run, you run. If I say stop, you stop. But there will be no need for you to stop, Blaire, because I *always* catch my victims."

My voice trembled when I spoke. "And what happens when you catch me?" I asked, half-afraid of his answer.

"Your body will get what it craves," he promised. His blue eyes connected with mine. "I have three rules: you cannot run to the road, and you cannot run back to the party. Do not shout or scream for help."

I nodded. I was both wanting to know what he would do when he caught me and also terrified of being around him much longer.

Bad things happened to stupid girls like me who went out on Halloween night. This was proof.

I would be lucky to survive.

"Do I get to know your name?" I blurted.

Where the fuck had that come from?

A wicked smile curved my captor's lips. Another thrill shot through me. "Striker." He tightened his hold on my neck, not cutting off my airflow, but still squeezing the sides. I knew his grip would leave bruises.

And that turned me on even more.

It was official. I needed serious, medical help.

He pressed a hot, searing kiss to my lips. It lasted a split second, but it felt like he branded my soul.

"Run."

Chapter Four

I wasn't stupid.

I didn't waste a second.

I spun around, and I ran.

Branches tore at my clothes - at my skin. They ripped at my fishnet stockings, revealing more of my legs.

I had never been more thankful that I wore boots than now. The terrain was rough and, at times, a bit slippery. If I'd worn heels or any other kind of shoes, I wouldn't be moving as easily as I was.

My lungs were screaming for air. I wasn't used to exercising, and running all over this hilly, rocky terrain was quickly wearing me out. All I ever did these days was inhale coffee and study.

I didn't think I'd actually exercised since I was required to take gym in high school.

I could feel Striker closing in on me. I knew he could catch me right now if he wanted to, but he was playing a game.

He *wanted* to chase me.

I hated that it excited me. I hated that *any* of this craziness was exciting me.

It was official. I was just as screwed up as the rest of my family.

Wanting this was as insane as the man behind me.

I dodged another rock that seemed to have popped up out of nowhere, almost falling flat on my face, but I caught my footing in time. I pushed harder. My hair-sprayed, colored hair was getting tangled from all the branches and leaves.

My legs were pleading for rest, shaking so badly that I was beginning to stumble. My lungs were screaming for air, a stitch in my side appearing. My eyes were burning from my makeup.

I was a mess, and yet, I didn't give up. I kept running. I refused to stop until this crazy son of a bitch caught me like he promised he would.

Somewhere along this run, I completely lost my fear. I wasn't even *afraid* anymore.

How crazy was that?

I could die tonight. I very well knew that, and yet, I wasn't fucking afraid.

All I wanted was for this insanely hot, crazy man to catch me.

My knees buckled just as my boot caught on a root. I shrieked, my hands going out in front of me to break my fall.

Striker was instantly there, his arm wrapping around me, flipping us so he took the brunt of the fall and I landed on his chest. His arms banded around me, anchoring my body down to his.

He'd caught me.

Not only that, but he had also stopped me from suffering a very rough fall.

I sucked in large, lung-fulls of air, trying to catch my breath and slow my racing heart. I could barely *breathe.*

Striker splayed his hand over my chest, his middle finger brushing my nipple. They instantly hardened. "Breathe in through your nose and exhale through your mouth," he commanded from beneath me.

Without hesitation, I obediently did as he said, and slowly, my breathing regulated, and my heart rate went back to mostly normal. My teeth were still aching with the phantom beat of my heart, but I didn't feel so deprived of oxygen now. I felt mostly okay again.

Though, my legs were a different story. They were *still* shaking from all the running I just did.

I squeaked in shock as Striker suddenly flipped us. I turned my head to the side so my face wouldn't be smashed into the dirt. The length of his body pressed against mine, and his hard cock pressed against my ass.

Wetness pooled between my thighs.

"I told you I always catch my victims," Striker breathed in my ear. I didn't stop the moan that crawled up my throat. "You gave a good chase, doll. I think it's time I give your body what it wants, don't you?"

Oh, God, yes, please.

"I'm not touching you until you tell me what you want, Blaire."

My cheeks warmed. The very few times I'd had sex with anyone, the lights were always off, I kept my shirt on, and I barely made a sound.

"Blaire," he whispered in a warning.

"Please," I blurted. I was *aching* for him. I didn't know how it was possible. I was putting it down to me being as crazy as the rest of my unstable family. "Please touch me," I begged him.

"*Just* touch you?" he asked, a teasing note in his voice. "I'm already touching you, doll."

I swallowed nervously. He sucked lightly at my earlobe, nipping gently at the tender flesh. I moaned, my ass thrusting up to rub against him. He growled softly, clamping his hand over my hip to anchor me to the ground. I whined in protest. "Tell me what you want, Blaire."

I squeezed my eyes shut. I was desperate. I knew I would never be able to satisfy myself if he let me go - not when I was this worked up.

"Please fuck me," I begged him.

"Good girl," he rumbled. My entire body sang at his praise.

He leaned up and rolled me to my back before pulling my jacket and shirt off of me, ripping my bra off right after. My nipples were hard, tight pebbles, my breasts heavy, aching for his touch, aching for his attention.

"Needy little thing, aren't you?" he hummed as he unzipped my boots and tossed them aside. His hands slid over my ripped fishnets before he got to the top of my thighs and ripped them off, shredding them. My panties were next - nothing left of them either once he was done. He slid my tutu off, leaving me bare on the ground.

The leaves were cold against my ass and back. The cooler night air danced over my heated flesh.

"Part your thighs," he commanded.

I instantly did as he asked. He sucked in a sharp breath. "Fuck, doll, you're soaked." He slid his fingers between my thighs, sliding my juices all over me, flicking my clit. I cried out in ecstasy, lifting my hips for more of his touch. "You've been *dying* to have my cock deep inside you, haven't you?"

I nodded, my cheeks warm despite the cold air. He leaned over me and took my lips in a hot, deep kiss. His tongue slid along mine, drawing a moan from the back of my throat. My hands clutched at his jacket, frustrated that his clothes were between us.

Then, his hand was between my legs.

I arched my back as he thumbed my clit, sliding two fingers inside of me at the same time. He leaned back on his knees, his eyes on my face as he fucked me with his fingers, his thumb never stopping that tormenting, slow, circular motion on my clit.

I was helplessly lost in him and everything he was doing to my body.

I never wanted him to stop.

"Yes, doll," he rasped as I tightened around him. I cried out his name, coming hard around his fingers right as he curled them a certain way, hitting something strange in me that had me detonating. My body trembled, white spots dancing across my vision.

When I floated back down to Earth, he was naked. Despite being lanky, he was toned, his muscles flexing as he moved. His abs rippled against the chill in the air.

Then, he was sinking deep inside of me. I didn't give a shit about a condom.

All I could focus on was his hard shaft inside of me, filling me up so much that it was almost painful.

But pain had never felt so damn good in my entire life.

He hooked one of my legs over his shoulder, curling the other around his back. He fucked me hard, relentlessly. I felt him deep inside, all the way to my lower belly. It hurt, but God, it hurt *so good.*

"You're so tight," he rasped. "*God, Blaire.*"

I clutched at his hot skin, lifting my hips to meet every rough, bruising thrust he made. His lips circled around my nipple, his other arm wrapping around my thigh so he could roughly grip my breast, squeezing the tender flesh before he pulled and twisted at the tight bud.

I screamed his name, my vision completely gone for a minute. He never stopped. He kept fucking me with hard, driving thrusts. The insides of my thighs were aching, but I never wanted it to end.

If he killed me tonight, I would honestly die a very satisfied woman.

Maybe that was his goal. I wasn't sure *what* his plan was for me.

But I knew one thing. I didn't give a fuck.

"Again," he growled once my vision cleared.

He reached between us and flicked my clit, setting me off again. I writhed on the ground, pushing against him, the stimulation too much to cope with, but he never stopped. He continued rubbing my clit in circles, sending me into orgasm after orgasm, my voice hoarse from screaming and pleading for him to both stop and keep going.

It felt so good - too good.

Finally, he shouted my name into the dark sky, coming inside of me. Then, he dragged me up from the ground, fisted his hand in my hair, and kissed me.

Chapter Five

My heart was thumping wildly in my chest. Striker was strangely running his hand over my tangled hair, occasionally pulling out leaves and sticks. His other arm was banded around me, anchoring my body to his.

Like the fucked up girl I'd become, I relished in what I was assuming was his affection.

He was still seated inside of me, still hard despite already having come. His heart was beating steadily, echoing inside my own chest that was pressed firmly against him.

"You're addicting, doll," he randomly spoke, jarring me from my thoughts.

Frowning, I leaned back to look at him. "Is that a bad thing?" I questioned him, unsure of where I stood now.

He tilted his head the tiniest bit, his eyes running over my face. "Actually, it might sort of work out in your favor."

I swallowed nervously. *Sort of work out in my favor.* What did that even mean?

"How so?" I questioned, nervous for his answer.

He ran his hand down my spine. I moaned, his touch turning me on all over again. A smirk tilted his lips for a split second before it disappeared again. "I want to keep you."

My breath hitched in my throat. My eyes widened in disbelief. "Keep me?" I squeaked. Why did that turn me on even more? Why was I *happy* with that answer?

He nodded. "Keep you."

I licked my suddenly dry lips. "What does that mean?" I quietly asked.

He gripped my ass in his hands, slowly moving me up and down on him. I moaned, my hands coming up to grip his shoulders. "It means you're mine, doll. We play games like this whenever I - or you - feel like it. I please your sexy, little body, and you please me by being my obedient, good girl."

His words turned me on even more. I linked my fingers behind his neck and began to ride him, sliding up and down his long, hard cock. His lips sucked at my neck and collar bone, no doubt leaving marks, but I didn't care.

He wanted to keep me.

That should terrify me.

It should have me running away from him, screaming for help.

But this man had me *craving* him. I didn't want to leave him.

Throw me in the loony bin. I didn't care. I was just as crazy for him, and even more, I was longing to belong completely to him - all at his mercy.

I wanted him to *own* me.

It didn't take long for me to come around him. My head rolled back on my shoulders, my eyes almost rolling to the back of my head.

Striker gripped my hair, pulling my face close to his. My body was still shaking from the effects of my orgasm, and I was a bit delirious from the pleasure rolling through my body. He ran his eyes over my face, a smile twitching at the corners of his lips.

"Want to play another game?"

I nodded. I wanted to play *any* game with this man, even ones that might get me killed.

"I want you to run again - naked this time." I moaned, moving on him again. He growled softly, stilling my hips. "And when I catch you, I want you to fight me, doll. Fight me hard every step of the way. And when I finally sink inside your tight, wet heat, *then* I want you to give yourself over to me completely and let yourself feel everything I do to this body that *I own.*"

He stood from the ground and set me on my feet. His eyes lit up with a dangerous glint that set my soul ablaze.

"Run, doll."

With a giggle I couldn't contain, I ran.

His cum was dripping down the inside of my thighs. I could hear him moving behind me. Sometimes, I could feel him so close that my body swayed back towards his. Other times, I knew he was staying back.

He was toying with me, and I was his all-too-willing puppet.

I was soaked - *drenched* - for him. Branches cut at my skin, making me bleed, and it *turned me on*. This man had awakened a darker side to my sexuality, made me crave something twisted - something I should be afraid to want.

But I wanted all of that dark, scary shit.

And I wanted it with *him - only* with him.

I wanted this man to corrupt me - to destroy my soul.

I wanted him to fuck me up so good that I didn't know a world outside of him.

Suddenly, his arms snagged around my waist. I bit my tongue so I wouldn't moan. He wanted me to fight him, and moaning was the exact opposite of that. I wanted him to overpower me, to take what solely belonged to him.

I thrashed in his grip, kicking him and elbowing him. I even bit him. He released a deep, dark, raspy chuckle when I did so that made my thighs even slicker as my own wetness mixed to combine with his cum.

I was a dirty, nasty mess, but I didn't care. I was a mess because of him.

"Fight me, doll," he rasped. He thrust against my ass as he dragged me down to the ground. I bucked back against him, trying to throw him off. When my ass rubbed his shaft, I barely bit back my moan. He was hard as steel, and my body was ready for him to fuck me - to claim the body that he owned.

He shoved me down onto the ground. I grappled at the dirt, going up on my knees, my ass now up in the air. "Knew you wanted it, you dirty slut," he growled as he gripped my hip, forcing my ass to stay in the air. "Sluts like you who run naked *deserve* to get fucked."

He drove up into me hard and fast without warning. A cry of pain mixed with my moan, and I gave into him, thrusting back on him as he fucked me from behind.

"Yes," he hissed through his teeth. "Just like a whore to beg to be fucked when she was just fighting me moments ago," he rasped. "Such a fucking whore, aren't you, Blaire?"

"Yes," I moaned. "Fuck me, please."

"Such a greedy, little bitch," he growled. I moaned his name.

God, yes. I was so fucking turned on. My thighs were slick, all of my wetness rubbing onto his thighs as well. I was spread far, my chest on the ground. He was driving into me with a force that hurt, but I was taking it just like the greedy whore he knew I was.

I never knew I was like this. I never knew I *wanted* this kind of thing. But like a true man, he aimed to please me, to give me what my subconscious had always secretly wanted.

"Striker," I whimpered, my fingers digging into the dirt.

He ran his hand over my spine, soothing me as my body began to shake. "Let go, doll. Give me *all* of you."

I screamed his name into the night air, my body shaking and trembling. He released a moment later, his thrusts slowing little by little until he was completely spent.

Then, he collapsed to the side of me and drew me into his arms, holding me tight against his chest. "You are something else, Blaire Wright," he finally uttered, his words soft.

I snuggled closer to him, a yawn spilling from my lips. He brushed his lips with mine, his lip ring cool against my face. "Stay here. I'm going to get our clothes, and then, I'll take you to my place."

I nodded, yawning again. "Promise you'll find me?" I sleepily asked him.

He smirked at me, warming my soul. "Doll, I've been following you for weeks. I'll find you anywhere."

Chapter Six

By the time Striker returned with our things - well, what was left of mine - I was shivering extremely hard - so hard my body ached - and my teeth were chattering. He had his jeans on along with his t-shirt, his shoes on his feet. Without a word, he slipped his leather jacket on me before he lifted me into his arms, holding me close to his chest.

“Give me a couple of minutes, and we’ll be at my car,” he assured me. “I’ll get some heat running for you.”

I nodded, my teeth still chattering too badly to form any kind of words. He tightened his hold on me, and despite him being lanky, he traipsed easily through the woods, climbing the rocky, hilly areas without any issue, even with me in his arms.

“How many times have you done this?” I quietly asked him once I could mostly speak again.

He glanced down at me before focusing back on where he was walking. “What - kidnapped my victims and fucked them?”

My heart clenched in my chest. I didn’t want to think of him doing this with anyone else. It actually hurt.

I bit my bottom lip and nodded.

He shook his head. “I kidnap them, yes. Normally, it’s a favor for my boss.” I frowned, confused. *Who in the hell did he work for?* “I toy with them, chase them, but I never fuck them.”

“Then, why me?” I softly asked him, my eyes running over his beautiful face. Whereas my makeup was smudged and ruined, his eyeliner was still perfect. I made a mental note to ask him later what brand he used.

“One, you weren’t a job for my boss,” he informed me. “I spotted you at the store with your friend, Amber while I was grocery shopping for the month.”

“Then why didn’t you just introduce yourself?” I quietly asked him, yawning right after. I would have gladly given this man every extra bit of my time.

He emerged from the woods with me in his arms and began walking through the now mostly empty car park. I hadn't realized we had been missing from the party for so long.

Guess it was true that time flew by when you were having fun.

"Not my style, doll."

I yawned again. He gently set my bare feet on the cool gravel beside an old, '69 Mustang. I watched, shivering, as he opened the door. Then, he placed his hand on my lower back and gently nudged me towards the passenger seat. Without a word, I sank down onto the plush leather, inhaling the scent of everything *him*.

I leaned my head back against the headrest, yawning tiredly. As soon as Striker was in the driver's seat and he had started the car, he turned the heat on, instantly beginning to warm my chilled bones.

"Better?" he asked, looking over at me through those electric, blue eyes, flicking his hair out of the way.

I nodded. He gripped the side of my neck in a tight, possessive grip and pulled my lips to his, kissing me so hotly that I contemplated climbing over onto his lap and riding his cock again.

"Get some rest. I don't live far."

I pushed up the middle console and laid across the seat, placing my head on his lap. Wordlessly, he draped his arm over me to grab the gear shift. I closed my eyes, enjoying the smell of him.

And oddly, I felt the safest I had in a *long* time.

I must have fallen asleep because the next thing I knew, I was being gently lifted from the car. I groaned in displeasure at being woken up.

If there was one thing I valued in life, it was sleep.

"Easy, doll," he rumbled. "It's just me."

That should have been alarming, but I was hooked on him. I craved his presence and his touch like an addict craved their next fix. I wasn't even ashamed about it.

I knew mental health issues ran in my family - had even sort of been prepared for it - and turns out, I seemed to be no exception.

I was weirdly okay with that.

I glanced around us, noticing that he had a small yard, his home surrounded by dense trees on all sides except for the opening for what seemed to be a long driveway. His house looked like a log cabin, and his porch expanded the width of the house. A porch swing blew in the breeze. It seemed oddly out of place with the man who lived here.

"You own this?" I asked him.

"Free and clear. Just pay taxes every year," he informed me as he stepped onto the porch and strode towards the front door. Without releasing me from his cradled hold, he unlocked the wooden door and pushed it open, carrying me inside.

It was warm and *very* cozy. The interior was done in dark colors, which fit him perfectly. A small fire was burning in the fireplace, a steel cage in front of it to keep any of the wood from falling out and hot coals from popping all over the floor.

"Let's get you cleaned up, doll," he murmured as he strode through his house. We stepped into what I immediately assumed was his room. It smelled like him, not to mention, the covers on the bed were haphazardly tossed aside - not made. And what appeared to be one of his socks was on the floor by the hamper.

He continued through his room and moved into an insanely large bathroom. A huge tub sat in the corner, and a large, glass shower stall was next to it. There were two sinks set into a large, marble counter.

The place was gorgeous.

"The tile is cold," he warned me as he set me on my tender feet. I winced once I was on my feet, the cuts

I had received while running naked now making themselves known.

He quickly stripped out of his clothes, revealing his beautifully sculpted body to me. I watched as he turned on the shower, and then, he turned to me. His eyes ran over me where I was huddled in his jacket, no doubt looking like a mess, and certainly not a hot one.

“Out of the jacket,” he ordered.

I obediently dropped the jacket from my shoulders, standing naked in front of him. My nipples pebbled into hard points, my core clenching as his eyes darkened.

He held his hand out to me, and I instantly placed my fingers on his palm, allowing him to wrap his large hand around them and pull me towards him. My body collided with his as I stumbled, and he banded his other arm around my waist, pressing my aching nipples against his hard chest.

“Still so eager even though I’ve basically fucked you into exhaustion,” he hummed.

My cheeks warmed. He took my lips in a hot kiss. I moaned into his mouth, my hands clawing at his back as I tried to get closer, desperately seeking out more of him.

"Later," he promised. "I need to get you cleaned up."

He led me into the warm shower. I sighed in contentment as soon as the hot water slid over my skin. It made the cuts on my body and feet sting, but I welcomed it. I was *so* eager for a shower.

Striker took his time bathing me, being gentle around the more tender parts of my body. Occasionally, he made a grunt of displeasure when he got to some of my worst bruises and markings, but otherwise, there was no sound between us.

Once my hair was washed and conditioned and I was clean, smelling just like him, he bathed himself, washing the eyeliner from beneath his eyes as he did so. I admired the way the muscles in his body flexed with each move he made.

And when he washed his cock, my mouth fucking salivated.

I wanted him deep in my throat.

"You like watching me?" he asked throatily, his blue eyes intent on my face.

I licked my lips, nodding my head in answer. He let the water wash the soap off his hard member, but he kept stroking, his eyes locked on me.

"On your knees," he finally commanded.

Greedily, I obeyed, dropping to my knees in front of him. He blocked the water from hitting me in my face and tapped the head of his cock against my lips. "Open, doll."

I parted my lips and took him into my mouth. He groaned, his eyes momentarily shutting before he released himself and fisted both of his hands in my hair. I wrapped one hand around the base of his shaft and used my other hand to cup his balls.

And he proceeded to fuck my mouth.

I moaned around him, rubbing my thighs together, rocking back and forth on my heels, desperate for him to be inside me, taking what now belonged to him.

"God, you're a greedy, desperate little whore," he growled, watching me.

I whined around his cock stuffing my mouth, sucking harder, tightening my hand around the base of him. He suddenly withdrew from my mouth, and using my hair, he gently tugged me to my feet.

Then, he spun me around and yanked at my hips. I quickly bent at a ninety-degree angle, my hands flat against the wall. I wiggled my ass in his direction, my body so sore, but yet, I couldn't resist him.

I moaned his name as he sank deep inside of me.

"Fuck, you're *soaked*," he growled, pounding in and out of me, fucking me like the little slut I was.

"All for you," I moaned.

I turned my head, watching as he leaned back some, watching as his cock disappeared inside of me over and over.

"Your pussy is so fucking greedy," he rasped. "It's swallowing my fucking cock, doll."

"Yes," I moaned. "Fuck me. *Please* fuck me."

He wrapped his hand around my throat, squeezing the sides of my neck so he wouldn't cut off my airflow. Then, he pulled me up so my back was flush with the front of his body, his other arm anchored around my hips as he kept scissoring in and out of me.

"Oh, God!" I cried out, my arms coming up behind me to clutch at the back of his neck. "Striker!"

"Yes, doll. Say my fucking name. Take this dick like the whore you are."

I came. Hard. I screamed, my body shaking in his hold. He roared my name as he came inside of me.

But he wasn't done yet.

Nope. He set me down, spun me around to face him, and then lifted me against the cold, shower wall before sinking deep inside of me again.

"You're tight, little body is fucking addicting, doll."

I grasped his face in my hands, leaning forward to take his lips. He rolled his hips as he drove back into me, making me gasp into our hot, wet kiss. His tongue tangled with mine. I clung to him, my tits bouncing every time he drove up into me.

"Tell me who you belong to," he demanded. "Whose fucking body is this?"

"Yours," I moaned, my eyes locked on his. One night, and I knew I would forever belong to this man. I didn't want it any other way. "I'm your dirty, greedy slut who wants to be endlessly fucked by you."

"*God*," he rasped, taking my lips again. "Your wish is my command, doll."

And he proceeded to fucking *ruin* me.

Chapter Seven

My legs weren't functioning correctly once we were done in the shower, so Striker dried me off before carrying my naked body to his bed. He then proceeded to put an antibiotic ointment on my wounds before putting lotion all over my body - something lavender scented.

It was soothing.

He laid on the bed behind me and pulled me into his arms, spooning me from behind. He rested his chin on the top of my head.

He was quiet. I chewed nervously on my bottom lip, my fingers absentmindedly trailing over his forearms. "Striker?" I softly spoke into the dark room.

He hummed in response.

I swallowed nervously, half afraid of his answer. "What happens in the morning?"

He tightened his hold on my naked body. "I'm taking you back to campus. You have class tomorrow afternoon."

I frowned, not liking the idea of being away from him. My mood instantly plummeted. "So, this was just one night of fun?" I asked, hating that my voice sounded so dejected.

He laughed softly. "I told you that your body belongs to me, Blaire." He slid his hand down my body, cupping me between my legs. I moaned, ready for him all over again. He slid my wetness around, the heel of his hand rubbing my clit. "You're *never* getting rid of me. Even if you try to run, I will find you *anywhere*."

"I don't want to run," I confessed. And I didn't. I wanted to stay with him forever.

He slipped a finger inside of me. I parted my legs further for him. "Good girl," he rumbled, praising me as he began to finger fuck me. "You're mine. You'll continue your education. You'll still hang out with your rather shitty friends." I frowned at his choice of words to describe my small group of friends. "And you'll be under my command." My pussy contracted around his finger at his words. "Like that, don't you, doll?"

"Yes," I moaned. I wasn't even ashamed. I sure as fuck wasn't going to deny it.

It didn't take long to get my overly sensitive body off, and once I was no longer trembling in his arms, he sucked my juices off his fingers before wrapping his arm back around me.

"Why did you call my friends shitty?" I asked him.

"Because real friends would not abandon the friend that clearly did not want to come to that party. They made you a promise to not abandon you tonight, did they not?"

I hated that he was right.

I sighed. "They have lives outside of me," I defended.

Striker sighed in irritation. I tensed. He smoothed his hand over my hip, relaxing me again. "I do not have time for people who abandon those they supposedly care about. In my world, your word is all you have. If you break that word, you can no longer be trusted."

"Your world?" I asked in confusion, rolling over to face him. His blue eyes locked on my green ones.

He nodded. "My world," he confirmed. "We're criminals, doll. We live on the other side of the law. Break your word to someone, and it could cost you your life."

A thrill shot through me at the thought of belonging to a man like him. He laughed softly.

"The thought of being with a criminal turns you on, doesn't it, doll?"

I nodded, knowing I had to answer. I was under his command now. He asked - I answered. He commanded - I followed orders.

I didn't want it any other way.

"And your family?" I quietly asked him, wondering where they all played into this.

"Murdered," he said, as if that was an everyday thing. My heart ached for him.

"I'm sorry," I said softly, meaning it. I knew what it was like to lose your family.

He shrugged. "It was a long time ago. I was a toddler. I don't remember much about them. The man I work for now took me under his wing and raised me. He's my family now."

I pressed a soft kiss to his chest, right above his heart. He sighed and cradled the back of my head, his other arm draping over my waist.

He tucked my head under his chin again. "Get some rest, doll. I'll wake you in enough time to get you fed before I take you back to campus."

I pressed my palms to his chest and closed my eyes, sighing in contentment.

That night, I lost my mind.

But I lost it in one of the most beautiful ways possible.

Chapter Eight

Striker leaned his back against his car and wound his arms around my waist, pulling me against him. He rested his chin on the top of my head. "What happened between us last night is no one else's business," he told me.

I nodded. "I know," I whispered, winding my arms around his waist. "Even if I could tell anyone, I wouldn't anyway. Last night was . . ." My voice trailed off.

Last night had been incredible.

And I didn't want to ruin the magic of the night before by telling my friends what had *really* transpired. Of course, I would have to tell them I had some pretty hot, out-of-this-world sex considering I had bruises on my neck from his grip, but they didn't need to know anything else.

Striker shucked the knuckle of his index finger under my chin, bringing my eyes up to his. "Be good today, you hear me? And stop letting your friends walk all over you. If you don't want to do something, don't do it. They don't own you."

I smiled. "No, they don't. You do."

He flashed me a wicked grin before leaning down to claim my lips with his. "Go on up and get some more sleep before class," he ordered.

"I will," I promised.

He kissed me again before releasing me. With a small smile, I turned on the heel of his oversized house slippers, heading inside my dorm building. I heard his car rumble back to life, and soon, he was driving away, heading back to his cabin to do work.

I already missed him.

With an exhausted sigh, I headed up the stairs to my dorm room. Amber was still in bed, but she looked away from her phone when I entered. Her eyes widened, and she quickly jumped down from the bed.

"Blaire!" she exclaimed. I winced at the volume of her voice. "Oh, my God. I thought you were missing!"

I blushed and shook my head, tucking my blonde hair behind my ear. "I, um, I was with someone."

She grinned at me, her eyes lighting up in amusement and pride. "You sneaky, little bitch," she laughed, a teasing note to her voice. She eyed the bruises on my neck. "Must have been some pretty fantastic sex."

I shrugged, my cheeks so hot I could feel it radiating from my skin. "Something like that," I mused. She knew I wasn't one to kiss and tell, anyway.

She laughed. "I know, I know. You don't kiss and tell." *See?* "You look exhausted. Why don't you get some more sleep before your first class this afternoon?"

I yawned with a nod and crawled up into my bed, snuggling beneath the covers in Striker's warm, long-sleeve shirt and his plaid pajama bottoms. Amber shut the light off for me, and within moments, I was knocked out again, dreams of Striker chasing me through the woods filling my subconscious mind.

My phone was beside me when I woke up - fully charged. And the LED light on it was flashing, letting me know that I had notifications.

Groggily, I picked up my phone, squinting at the screen. I noted that I had about two hours before I had to be to class. That was enough time to shower, get dressed, hunt down food, and get to my first lecture of the day.

Rise and shine, doll.

My mood instantly brightened at the sight of Striker's text. I'd barely been out of his presence, and I still craved all of his attention.

I quickly saved his number before I texted him back.

I'm up. Barely - but I'm up.

I watched as three bubbles appeared on the screen, indicating he was texting me back. My heart warmed. He wasn't wasting time, playing around with me like so many other guys were prone to do.

Get a shower. Get some food. I'll come see you after your classes are over.

I sent a simple heart emoji in answer before I slipped off the bed and grabbed my towel and my toiletries, heading across the hall to get a shower. As soon as the water touched my skin, I was instantly transported back to my time in the shower with Striker, how he fucked my mouth, drove up into me from behind, claimed my body as his as he held me against the shower wall.

I slid my hand between my legs.

I tilted my head back, rolling my nipple between my thumb and index finger, the heel of my hand rubbing over my clit as I slid two fingers into my slick heat. I barely bit back a moan of Striker's name as I envisioned him between my legs, his tongue inside me, his mouth sucking on my clit.

It took almost no time at all to come all over my fingers. I was panting. And even though I'd gotten myself off, my body still craved more.

This evening couldn't fucking come fast enough. I *needed* Striker.

After I got out of the shower, I traipsed back to my room, instantly checking my phone for a text from Striker before I even got dressed.

His text was there, waiting for me.

I'm assuming by the length of your shower, you're fucking that pretty little cunt with your fingers.

My cheeks burned. *How did he know?*

Do you have a camera in my room?

His answer was immediate.

Something like that.

I looked around, seeing if I could find it, but I didn't spot anything. I frowned in confusion.

Don't bother looking. You won't find it. How was your shower?

I sighed. He was good at this. He'd been monitoring me for weeks, and I had no idea. Never even *thought* of the possibility of a stalker. I'd felt completely safe.

In a way, I guess I kind of had been. Striker didn't want to hurt me.

Instead, he just wanted to claim me - own me.

I was an extremely willing prisoner.

A bit disappointing. I miss you.

Those bubbles popped up on the screen again.

I'll take care of you when I see you this evening. Get dressed. Get some food. Now.

I smiled.

Yes, sir.

My brain felt fried. I was exhausted. My stomach was rumbling for food again, and I was missing Striker like crazy.

I squeaked in shock when I pushed open the door to my dorm room, finding Derreck balls deep inside Amber. My cheeks warmed in embarrassment. They had been dating for a while now, but I'd never caught them fucking before. Sure, I'd caught them in many other compromising positions, but normally, at least *one* of them would still have clothes on.

"Want to join them?" Striker whispered in my ear from behind, his hands sliding over my hips. It didn't even seem like Amber and Derreck had noticed me. "Your nipples are fucking hard as hell, doll." He wasn't kidding. The sight of Amber and Derreck fucking was a huge turn-on.

Striker gently nudged me further into the room, shutting the door behind him. Amber moaned loudly, crying out Derreck's name. And he didn't stop. He pushed her leg higher, fucking her harder.

Striker slid his hand between my legs. "Fuck, you're so wet you've soaked your leggings."

I bit back a moan at the feeling of his palm sliding against me through my clothes. Striker gripped my chin, keeping my eyes locked on Amber and Derreck. "Watch, doll."

I obediently did as he said. He moved back from me, and then a couple moments later, he pulled my shirt over my head, my bra following next. Then, my soaked leggings and panties went to the floor. "On the bed," Striker commanded.

I turned to face him, not biting back my moan this time when I saw him. He was naked, and his cock was hard and ready for me.

I crawled onto the bed.

"Joining in on the fun?" Derreck asked as Amber cried out again.

"She's got a kinky ass side to her," Striker told him as he crawled up the bed after me. He grabbed my ankle and flattened me on the bed before sinking into me.

I arched my back, crying out his name. Striker hooked both legs over his shoulders and braced his hands on either side of me, proceeding to fuck me hard and deep, his hips pistoning back and forth as he took me in a controlled, almost savage-like way.

"God, your so fucking wet, baby," Derreck rasped as he leaned over Amber, sucking on the skin of her neck.

"Striker," I moaned, clutching at his arms, my nails clawing at his skin.

"I told you I'd take care of you," Striker told me. My legs fell from his shoulders only to hook over his arms, spreading me wider. "Your hot, tight pussy is *begging* for this cock."

"Yes," I whimpered. "Oh, God, yes."

Striker leaned down, stretching my legs further back to the point it hurt. I parted my lips for him, inviting his tongue in as I clenched around his shaft, already coming. I screamed, my hands clawing at his shoulders, drawing blood as I broke the skin.

Suddenly, he pulled out, making me feel empty, and spun me around so I was forced to connect my eyes with Amber's. Derreck was drilling into her from behind. Her tits were swaying back and forth, her mouth parted, her eyes glazed with pleasure.

Striker slammed into me. I screamed. My head fell forward, exposing the back of my neck to Striker. "Oh, God, you fuck so good," I whimpered.

"Your body was *made* for me," Striker rasped.

"Derreck," Amber whimpered.

"Take it, baby," he growled at her. "You begged for this. You begged me to fuck you until you couldn't walk."

I came again. Striker wrapped his hand around my throat, dragging my body up like he had the night before. Amber cried out, her eyes on us as Striker fucked me hard, fucked me so deep I felt him in my lower stomach.

"Come," Striker growled in my ear. "Make that pussy come all over my cock."

He pinched my nipples, and I fucking lost it. I fought against his hold, trying to ground myself as I came so hard I momentarily completely lost my vision. He tightened his hold on my neck and wrapped his arm across my tits, anchoring me to him as he continued to screw up inside of me, sending me spiraling over and over into multiple orgasms. I didn't even have time to recover from one before he was spinning me headfirst into another one.

When the black spots cleared from my vision, Striker was running his hand over my body, whispering soothing words into my ears. I slowly began to make them out as the ringing in my ears disappeared.

"Breathe, doll," Striker whispered. "I've got you. Breathe."

I sucked in lungful after lungful of air, gasping. Amber was sprawled over the bed, and Derreck was rubbing her back as she tried to catch her breath.

"I think I'm going to be sick," I moaned.

Derreck jumped off the bed and grabbed the trashcan just in time. I emptied my stomach, my body too hot and too worked up to keep anything down.

"Easy now," Striker murmured. "You're panicking. I need you to breathe."

Was I panicking?

"Breathe," he softly coaxed, never stopping the movement of his hand over my body. His other hand was still latched around my throat, somehow grounding me - not making me feel constricted. "It's okay. Just breathe."

I sank into his hold, no longer able to hold myself up. He drew me down to the mattress and wrapped my sweaty body up in his hold. "Good girl," he praised. "There you go."

"Nap," I mumbled, my eyes falling shut.

"Sleep, doll."

Chapter Nine

Striker flashed me a grin as I slid my hand over the crotch of his jeans. We'd gone on a late-night drive, but I couldn't keep my hands off of him.

He'd been gone for two days on a job, and our contact had been limited due to the kind of job he had to do.

I'd missed him – desperately.

"You're a needy little thing, aren't you?" he asked me, his hand circling my wrist, but he didn't stop me from touching him.

"Yes," I whispered, trailing my lips along his neck. He groaned softly, his hand leaving my wrist to grip my hair, pulling lightly on my scalp. I moaned. "I missed you, and I still haven't had enough of you."

He'd fucked me for *hours* after he picked me up from my dorm and took me back to his place. Still, it hadn't been enough. Where Striker was concerned, I was fucking insatiable.

He grabbed my hand when I moved to undo his belt buckle. "Wait." I frowned at him. I knew he wanted me just as badly. His jeans were about to fucking burst. So, why was he stalling? "I need to ask you something before we fuck again."

"What?" I asked him. Now, I was really confused. Nothing stopped this man from taking what belonged to him.

"I want you to marry me - this weekend. We'll elope. I'll fly us out to Vegas. Have a shotgun wedding."

My lips parted in surprise. My soul warmed. Tears glistened in my eyes as I stared at him.

"You want to marry me?" I croaked.

He nodded. "You're mine, Blaire. No one else will ever touch you again. They can watch me fuck you," which was something Derreck and Amber had joined in on a lot after that first time, "but they can *never* touch you. I'll fucking kill them. I want to own you in every possible way there is to own you."

"Really?" I breathed. It seemed too good to be true. This man actually wanted to *keep* me - for that long?

He nodded in answer as he pulled off on a random dirt road, shoving his car into first before turning to look at me. "Yes. I need to know I own you in every way there is."

"Yes," I breathed. "You already own me, Striker Benjamin. I'm completely yours."

He grabbed the back of my neck and yanked my mouth to his, kissing me hotly and deeply. All while he kissed me, he undid his belt buckle and unsnapped his jeans, pulling his cock out. I hiked my dress up, and since I didn't have panties on, I climbed on top of him, sinking down on him.

"Yes," I moaned.

Striker ripped my dress over my head, baring my body to him. "God, you have perfect tits," he rumbled. He leaned forward and pulled one nipple into his mouth, sucking greedily as he roughly gripped the other one, pressing into the bruises already there.

My man loved roughly, and I relished in his brutal touch.

"Fuck me, Striker," I pleaded.

He gripped my hips and shoved up into me, lifting my body up and down his hard shaft as he did so. My tits bounced in his face, and I pulled at my nipples before I gripped his head and buried his face between my breasts, pulling at his hair.

"God, you're so fucking needy," he rasped, sucking on the skin of my chest.

"I'm greedy for your cock," I moaned. "If I could live with you inside me all day every day, I fucking would."

"Such a whore," he rasped, biting roughly at my skin.

I screamed his name, coming hard just as blue and white lights lit up the night sky. Striker lifted his head from my chest, cursing. "Shit," he growled. "Hold on, doll."

He took off down the dirt road, and those lights followed us. I became wetter at the thrill of the crime, at us being chased by a cop, and Striker hissed. "Ride me," he growled. "Fuck me. Take what you need from me, Blaire. My woman is *not* going to be left unsatisfied."

I did as he commanded, bouncing up and down on his steel cock, taking whatever I wanted from him. I was crying out his name, moaning, my head buried in his shoulder as I fucked him, twisting my hips, my pussy soaking his dick.

His phone rang, but I didn't stop, even after he answered it. "Yeah?" Striker gritted as he took a sharp turn. I clung to him, crying out as I came around him again. But I wasn't nearly done.

"Sending two men to come block that officer from you," a man's voice came through the line. "Keep heading home. I'm accessing his database now and wiping your plate from the system."

"Got it," Striker said. "Fuck, doll," he rasped as I clenched around him again.

"Are you *fucking* someone while driving?" the man on the phone asked incredulously.

Striker smirked. "More like she's fucking me, boss."

"Jesus Christ," he swore. "Touch base when you get home."

The call ended. "You are such a nasty slut," Striker laughed, down-shifting to take a sharp curve.

"I like people," I panted, "knowing who I," I moaned, "belong to."

He pressed a kiss to my shoulder before focusing his eyes back on the road. "I'll reward you for it when we get your cute ass home."

I reached between us and rubbed my clit, coming all over him once again.

Once we got home, Striker got out of the car with me still wrapped around him. He set me on the hood of his Mustang, the metal hot against my back, but I didn't care. It only stimulated me more.

"I believe I said I would reward you, correct?"

"Yes," I whispered, reaching for him.

He pulled his shirt over his head and kicked out of the rest of his clothes before he gripped my breasts, bruising me even more as he pinned me to the hood, his hips thrusting back and forth, his still drenched cock driving in and out of me.

He fucked me like a man starved - like a savage.

"Striker!" I cried out, my back arching.

"This weekend - Vegas," he rasped. "And then, I'm knocking you up."

I came again at his words. He growled. "I might," I sucked in air, "already be," I whined as he rubbed my clit, "pregnant."

"Good," he rumbled.

Headlights swept into the yard. A black SUV emerged. Striker cursed and pulled out of me. I whined in protest, reaching for him, not near done.

He gathered me close and pressed a kiss to my swollen lips before he pulled his shirt over my head, hiding my body. "Business. I have to handle this. Then, I'll finish taking care of you, you hear me?"

I nodded, pouting at him. He shook his head before he kissed me again. "Stay," he ordered. Then, he yanked his jeans up his legs and strode to the SUV, his upper body bare.

An older man stepped out of the driver's seat. His hair was black, sprinkled with spots of gray. He looked at me before looking back at Striker.

"She trustworthy?"

Striker nodded. "Probably the most loyal person I fucking know." My soul warmed. Striker really did trust me that much. After all, my entire world revolved around him, and I hadn't breathed a word to anyone of how we met.

It was our dirty, fucked-up secret.

They walked over to me. Striker placed a possessive hand over my bare thigh once he was beside me again. The man ran his eyes over me. "She the one on the phone call?"

I blushed. Striker nodded. "She is."

The man held his hand out to me, an amused smirk tilting his lips. "Lorenzo Rossi. You are?"

I shyly shook his hand. "Blaire Wright," I said softly.

"Soon to be Benjamin," Striker informed the man. "She agreed to marry me tonight. We'll be wedded over the weekend in Vegas."

Lorenzo smiled. "Welcome to the family, Blaire. Anyone who's bold enough to fuck the driver while being chased by a cop is definitely welcome into this family."

I tucked my hair behind my ear, my cheeks burning red. I glanced at Striker. His eyes ran over my face before he reached up and ran his hand over my hair. I glanced back at Lorenzo. "Thank you."

He nodded once and looked at Striker. "We have some things to discuss. Got another job coming up for you next week. You can bring your wife along."

"Come inside," Striker told him. Without a word to me, Striker lifted me against his chest and carried me inside the house, setting me on the couch. He strode into the kitchen as Lorenzo took a seat on the other couch. In the light, I could see that his suit was immaculate and definitely expensive. The man obviously had a shit ton of money, but he flaunted his, unlike Striker who preferred to live humbly.

Striker stepped into the living room, handing me a bottle of water before he handed a beer to Lorenzo. "Drink," he told me. "You're dehydrated." He took a seat next to me. "What's this job entail?" he asked Lorenzo.

After I guzzled down the bottle of water, I rested my head on Striker's shoulder. Silently, he draped one of the blankets on the back of the couch around me before he wrapped his arm around my shoulder, listening as Lorenzo told him about the job. I closed my eyes, yawning quietly. Striker tightened his arm around me in response.

I vaguely made out some things like a hit, money, and some other terms, but I was too tired to care. Not to mention, this wasn't any of my business. I would be along for the trip, nothing else.

Striker told me what I needed to know, and if I didn't need to know it, then it wasn't any of my concern. He took care of me, and that was all I cared about.

Epilogue

Getting married in Vegas was honestly a dream. We spent the entire weekend there, not to mention, we spent every waking moment together, which infinitely pleased me. Striker took my body to all new heights, and he also made me feel like a princess the entire weekend.

I'd bought clothes I'd never be able to afford on my own. He took me to some of the best restaurants apparently known to man.

And the drunken nights were even better. Well, I was drunk. Striker stayed sober. And apparently, I was slutty as fuck when I was drunk. I almost stripped in the bar, but Striker paid the bouncer and took me to the bathroom, fucking me for almost two hours - fucked me to the point he had to *carry* me back to our hotel.

Now, we were back to reality, but my friends were coming over along with some of Striker's colleagues to celebrate Striker and I getting hitched.

And I had a surprise for my husband.

I smiled as I stared down at the two pregnancy tests on the counter. I still needed to get checked by a doctor, but I was pretty sure I was pregnant. My breasts had been tender, and I was pretty nauseated in the mornings.

Striker leaned against the door jamb, his arms crossed over his chest. "What do you got there?" he stood up straight and peered over my shoulder. Then, he spun me around, his hands clamped over my upper arms. He ran his eyes over me, settling on my belly. "You're pregnant?" he breathed.

I shrugged. "Seems so." A smile tugged at my lips.

He crushed his mouth to mine before he lifted me onto the bathroom counter and shoved my dress up. Per his rules, I had no panties on, giving him easy access to me whenever I needed to be fucked. Striker always aimed to take care of me.

Within a split moment, he was deep inside of me. He pinned my arms behind my back, making my chest thrust out. His lips worked with mine, but unlike every other time we fucked, he took his time with me, treasuring me.

I cried as he took my body, loving me in a way only he could.

"God, you have no idea how fucking happy I am right now," he rasped.

He kissed my tears away as I came hard around him. This time, he didn't hold himself back, and he came with me, holding me close to his chest as he whispered dirty secrets of what he would do to my body as it grew to accommodate our child.

Striker was coddling the hell out of me, and I was loving every bit of it. Not to mention, he was now *super* overprotective. And it didn't annoy me. It made me feel extremely safe.

So, when Amber squeezed me into a tight hug, basically jumping on me, I only giggled when Striker gently pulled me back from her, frowning at my best friend.

"Easy with her, yeah?" he told Amber, flattening his hand over my belly.

She gasped, her eyes going wide. "You're pregnant?!" she squealed, jumping in place so she wouldn't launch herself at me. Derreck helped by keeping a restraining hand on her shoulder.

I laughed. "According to the tests I took this morning, yes," I confirmed. "I still need to see the doctor, though."

Striker only grunted. He knew as well as I did that I was very much pregnant.

She hugged me more gently this time, taking note of the overprotective man still holding me. "Oh, I'm so happy for you, Blaire. You're going to make an amazing mom."

My throat closed up with tears. I squeezed her, sniffling as I tried to keep them from spilling over onto my cheeks. "Sorry," I croaked, reaching up to swipe at the tear that rolled down my cheek. "I'm a bit emotional."

Amber's smile widened. "*Definitely* pregnant."

I blushed.

Striker led me inside. Once I was sitting on the couch, he disappeared into the kitchen. Derreck followed him. Instantly, my friends surrounded me, dying for the details on Vegas. With a smile continuously on my face, I gave them all the details of the restaurants, the views, the food, our hotel, and our wedding. They hung onto my every word. The only thing I left out were the extremely hot moments with Striker.

Eventually, Striker's friends showed up. My husband took a seat beside me, handing me a bottle of water, leaning over to take my lips in a slow, hot kiss that had me yearning for him.

"Later," he whispered against my lips, the promise of sensuality in his eyes.

Our afternoon went smoothly. There was lots of laughter and plenty of food. Striker hardly left my side, and I basked in his attention.

I loved how attentive he was to me, especially now.

Eventually, Melanie, Jess, Kylie, and Amber had to head back to campus to get ready for class the next morning. I gave them hugs, promising to meet them at the coffee shop on campus for lunch the next day.

Then, it was just me, Striker, and his friends.

Striker slid his hand over my thigh as he talked to one of the guys about the upcoming trip. Apparently, he was coming with us. I was barely listening though. All I could focus on was Striker's hand slowly inching further up my thigh.

I leaned my head on his shoulder, bringing my lips close to his ear. "Fuck me," I whispered, my words a plea. I'd gone too long without him.

He snapped his head around to me, abruptly stopping mid-sentence. "Please," I begged him.

"Now?" he asked, double-checking, his eyes darkening as he slid his hand fully between my legs.

I parted them, revealing I still wasn't wearing panties. His blue eyes darkened even further as he brushed his fingers over my wet slit.

I nodded. "In front of them," I boldly spoke aloud, my eyes never leaving his startling blue irises.

"Fuck," he growled. He grabbed a handful of my hair and took my lips in a rough kiss that stole my breath. My nipples peddled beneath my bra, desperate for his rough touch.

"Jesus Christ," one of the guys uttered.

"Bout to be a lot more than that." I looked up at the sound of Lorenzo's voice as Striker sucked on the lobe of my ear. I closed my eyes, moaning as I clutched at this head. "His wife has a thing for exhibitionism."

I moaned as Striker slid his hands up my hips, pulling my dress with it. Finally, he pulled it over my head before unsnapping my bra, tossing it to the floor.

"You have got to be the neediest woman I've ever met in my life," Striker growled.

"Fuck me," I begged him. I *needed* him inside of me.

With a growl, Striker roughly drove his fingers inside of me. I mewled, my back arching, my legs spreading wider to reveal all that glistening, pink skin down below that was solely his. He was the only man that would ever touch me like this ever again.

"Such a slut," Striker rasped, his eyes on my face as he fucked me with his fingers. I moaned at his words, moving my hips to rub more against his hand, drenching his fingers.

"So wet for me," he praised.

"More," I pleaded.

Never one to deny me of what I needed - not when it came to sex - Striker pulled his cock from his black sweats and slid deep inside of me. I clutched at his shoulders, winding my legs around his hips as he quickly brought me to the edge.

"You're mine," he rasped, fucking me harder.

I screamed his name.

WANT MORE OF STRIKER AND BLAIRE?

https://mybook.to/unexpectedstpatday

PLEASE LEAVE A REVIEW!

I would love to hear your thoughts on the book!

Please leave a review on Amazon. I would love to see your thoughts, whether you liked it or disliked it.

Link:
https://mybook.to/unexpectedhalloween

FOLLOW T.O. SMITH

Facebook:
https://www.facebook.com/authortosmith

Facebook group:
https://www.facebook.com/groups/TOSmith

TikTok: https://www.tiktok.com/@tiffwritesromance

Instagram:
https://www.instagram.com/authortosmith/

Twitter: https://twitter.com/tiffwritesbooks

Amazon:
https://www.amazon.com/author/tosmith

Website: https://tosmithbooks.com

OTHER BOOKS BY T.O. SMITH

Website: https://tosmithbooks.com

Amazon:
https://www.amazon.com/author/tosmith

https://www.patreon.com/tiffwritesromance

ABOUT THE AUTHOR

T.O. Smith believes in one thing - a happily ever after.

Her books are fast-paced and dive straight into the romance and the action. She doesn't do extensively drawn-out plots. Normally, within the first chapter, she's got you - hook, line, and sinker.

She is a top-100 international best-selling author in three categories: Romantic Action & Adventure, Thriller & Suspense Action Fiction, and Action & Adventure Fiction (Kindle Store).

As a writer of various different genres of romance, a reader is almost guaranteed to find some kind of romance novel they'll enjoy on her page.

T.O. Smith can be found on Facebook, Instagram, Twitter, and now even TikTok! She loves interacting with all of her readers, so follow her!

Printed in Poland
by Amazon Fulfillment
Poland Sp. z o.o., Wrocław

27045812R00052